Sometimes It's BRIGHT

Annie Ruygt

BOYDS MILLS PRESS

AN IMPRINT OF BOYDS MILLS & KANE

New York

For my parents,
Andrea and Rebecca,
who help me see my brightness

For information about permission to reproduce selections
from this book, please contact permissions@bmkbooks.com.

Boyds Mills Press
An imprint of Boyds Mills & Kane,
a division of Astra Publishing House
boydsmillspress.com
Printed in China

ISBN: 978-1-68437-982-8 (hc) • 978-1-63592-375-9 (eBook)
Library of Congress Control Number: 2020932441

First edition
10 9 8 7 6 5 4 3 2 1

Design by Barbara Grzeslo
The text is set in KG Neatly Printed.
The illustrations are done in watercolor and
colored pencil on Arches hot press paper.

What is that magic,
sparkling and sheer?

I wish I could catch it

and bring it down here.

Sometimes it's
BIG.

Sometimes it's bright!

Sometimes it's on stage on opening night.

It can be loud,
and it can go far.

But it can fade fast
and flee to the stars.

It's right there beside me.

Then, it is not.

How can I find it?

Can it be bought?

If I take note
and share what I see . . .

Wait, there it is!

It's coming from me.

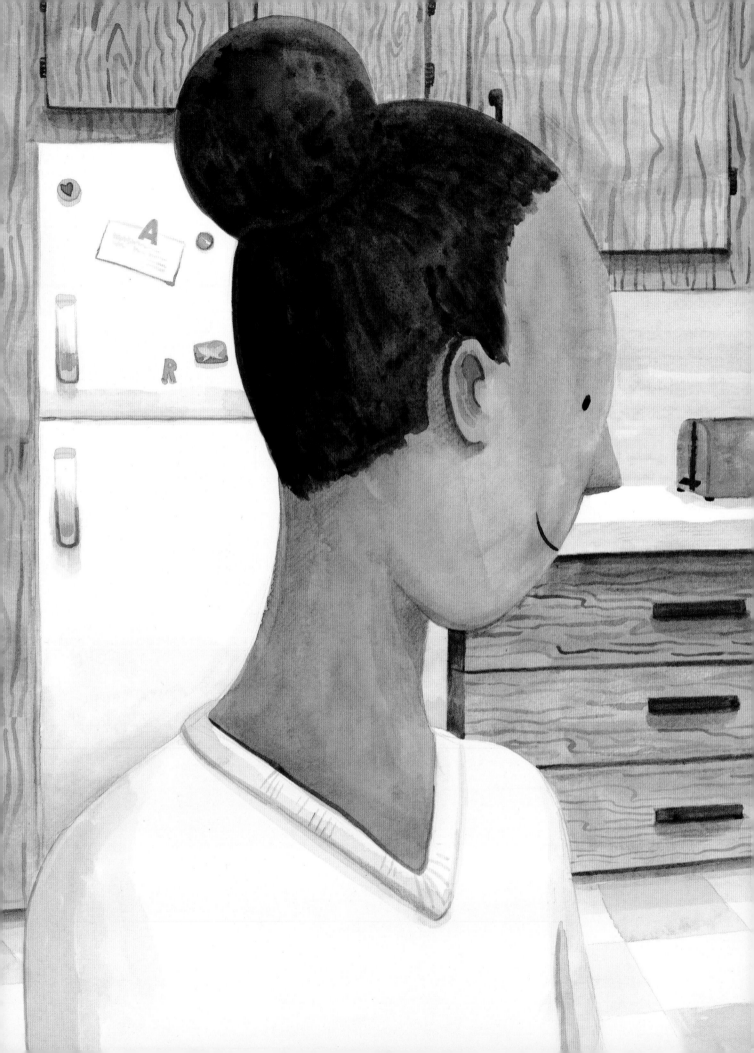

Sometimes it's quiet,
sometimes it's small.

But, boy, does it sparkle and dance down the hall.

The magic's in me!
I can draw! I can sing!

I shine brightest
when I do my thing.